Alexandria Public Library
P.O. Box 67
Alexandria, OH 43001-0067

Team Spirit

THE JACKSONVILLE JAGUARS

BY
MARK STEWART

Content Consultant
Jason Aikens

Chicago, Illinois

Norwood House Press
P.O. Box 316598
Chicago, Illinois 60631

For information regarding Norwood House Press, please visit our website at: www.norwoodhousepress.com or call 866-565-2900.

PHOTO CREDITS:
All photos courtesy of Getty Images except the following:
Author's Collection (9, 34 left); Topps, Inc. (14, 21, 23 top, 35 bottom left & right, 43); Black Book Partners Archive (28, 40 top); Matt Richman (48 top).
Cover Photo: Doug Benc/Getty Images
Special thanks to Topps, Inc.

Editor: Mike Kennedy
Designer: Ron Jaffe
Project Management: Black Book Partners, LLC.
Research: Evan Frankel
Special thanks to: Tom Majdanics and the Zanghetti/Phillips Family

LIBRARY OF CONGRESS CATALOGING-IN-PUBLICATION DATA

Stewart, Mark, 1960-
  The Jacksonville Jaguars / by Mark Stewart ; content consultant Jason Aikens.
     p. cm. -- (Team spirit)
  Includes bibliographical references and index.
  Summary: "Presents the history, accomplishments and key personalities of the Jacksonville Jaguars football team. Includes timelines, quotes, maps, glossary and websites"--Provided by publisher.
  ISBN-13: 978-1-59953-209-7 (library edition : alk. paper)
  ISBN-10: 1-59953-209-3 (library edition : alk. paper) 1. Jacksonville Jaguars (Football team)--History--Juvenile literature. I. Aikens, Jason. II. Title.
  GV956.J33S84 2008
  796.332'640975912--dc22
                                                          2008012720

© 2009 by Norwood House Press.
Team Spirit™
All rights reserved.
No part of this book may be reproduced without written permission from the publisher.

•

The Jacksonville Jaguars is a registered trademark of Jacksonville Jaguars, Ltd.
This publication is not affiliated with the Jacksonville Jaguars, Ltd., The National Football League, or The National Football League Players Association.

Manufactured in the United States of America.

COVER PHOTO: The Jaguars celebrate a victory during the 2006 season.

Table of Contents

CHAPTER	PAGE
Meet the Jaguars	4
Way Back When	6
The Team Today	10
Home Turf	12
Dressed for Success	14
We Won!	16
Go-To Guys	20
On the Sidelines	24
One Great Day	26
Legend Has It	28
It Really Happened	30
Team Spirit	32
Timeline	34
Fun Facts	36
Talking Football	38
For the Record	40
Pinpoints	42
Play Ball	44
Glossary	46
Places to Go	47
Index	48

SPORTS WORDS & VOCABULARY WORDS: In this book, you will find many words that are new to you. You may also see familiar words used in new ways. The glossary on page 46 gives the meanings of football words, as well as "everyday" words that have special football meanings. These words appear in **bold type** throughout the book. The glossary on page 47 gives the meanings of vocabulary words that are not related to football. They appear in ***bold italic type*** throughout the book.

Meet the Jaguars

How long should it take for a brand-new football team to become a championship *contender*? Five years? Ten years? The Jacksonville Jaguars did it in *two* years. At the end of their second season, the Jaguars came within two touchdowns of going to the **Super Bowl**. Their fans cheered them on every step of the way.

The Jaguars became a winning team by finding players who did their jobs with pride. They helped each other when the going got tough. They trusted their coaches and believed that good guys can finish first. They have played this way ever since, and the results have been *sensational*.

This book tells the story of the Jaguars. They built a *tradition* of success faster than any **professional** football team in history. By putting the good of the team first, the players have created an atmosphere where football is fun—and winning is *contagious*!

The Jaguars congratulate Fred Taylor after a touchdown during a 2007 game.

Way Back When

When the **National Football League (NFL)** announced in 1991 that it would soon be adding two new teams, no one thought that Jacksonville, Florida would get one. It was smaller than the other cities hoping for a team. It also had a lot of college football fans. Would they also support an NFL team? The league believed that the people of Jacksonville would. The NFL announced

that the Jaguars would be its 30th team. The fans "thanked" the NFL and team owner J. Wayne Weaver by buying 55,000 **season tickets**.

The Jaguars played their first season in 1995. They were led by coach Tom Coughlin. Their first **draft pick** was offensive lineman Tony Boselli. The Jaguars also drafted a running back named James Stewart, traded for quarterback

LEFT: Tom Coughlin discusses a play with Mark Brunell.
RIGHT: The great receiving duo of Jimmy Smith and Keenan McCardell.

Mark Brunell, and signed receiver Jimmy Smith as a **free agent**. Although they won only four games their first year, the Jaguars had built a good foundation for the future.

That future arrived sooner than anyone expected. The Jaguars played well early in the 1996 season, though they lost a lot of close games. Then Jacksonville began winning. Brunell led the NFL with 4,367 passing yards. Smith and newcomer Keenan McCardell both caught more than 80 passes. Running back Natrone Means was unstoppable in the final two months of the year. Jacksonville fans watched in amazement as their team won its last five games and made it to the **playoffs**.

The Jaguars kept on winning and advanced all the way to the championship game of the **American Football Conference (AFC)**. They lost to the New England Patriots 20–6, but the game was very close until the end. Still, the Jaguars almost made it to the Super Bowl in just their second season!

The team made it to the playoffs again the next three seasons in a row. In 1999, the Jaguars had the NFL's best record at 14–2. Their only losses were to the Tennessee Titans. Jacksonville returned to the **AFC Championship** game. Unfortunately, the team missed its chance to reach the Super Bowl with a third loss to the Titans. It was a painful defeat for many reasons. The Jaguars actually led the game but let their advantage slip away in the second half.

Despite the loss to Tennessee, Jacksonville remained a confident team. The Jaguars had an excellent defense, thanks to leaders Kevin Hardy, Tony Brackens, Carnell Lake, Marcus Stroud, Bryce Paup, and Donovin Darius. Meanwhile, running back Fred Taylor had joined the offense. He would become the greatest player in team history.

The Jaguars rebuilt their team in the early years of the 21st *century*. Jack Del Rio took over as coach and tried different combinations of players to find a winning *formula*. The Jaguars had some losing seasons, but they never lost their winning attitude. It would not be long before they were enjoying success in the playoffs again.

LEFT: Fred Taylor, Jacksonville's top runner and a respected leader.
ABOVE: A souvenir pin from the 1990s.

The Team Today

The career of the normal NFL player is very short. The Jaguars have been lucky because many of their top stars from the 1990s continued to play well for 10 seasons or more. Fred Taylor and Jimmy Smith were still going strong in 2005, when Jacksonville won 12 games and returned to the playoffs.

Two years later, the Jaguars made another run for the Super Bowl. Maurice Jones–Drew had joined Taylor to give the team a great running attack. Quarterback David Garrard and receiver Reggie Williams were the stars of the passing game. The leaders on defense were Mike Peterson, Rashean Mathis, and Reggie Nelson. Jacksonville raced to an 11–5 record in 2007—and a thrilling victory in the playoffs against the Pittsburgh Steelers.

The Jaguars know how to build a winner. Right after the 2007 season, they began adding new pieces to their puzzle, including speedy receiver Jerry Porter. The names and faces of the Jaguars may change, but the winning spirit remains the same.

David Garrard hands the ball to Fred Taylor. They were two of the key offensive players for the 2007 Jaguars.

Home Turf

The Jaguars play in Jacksonville Municipal Stadium. It is located in downtown Jacksonville, near the St. Johns River. The stadium was built in 1995 on the site of the old Gator Bowl, a famous college football stadium. Part of the Gator Bowl was kept to blend in with the new stadium. The annual Gator Bowl game is still played in the stadium.

When Jacksonville found out the Jaguars were coming, the city started construction of the team's stadium. It opened in time for the club's first game of the regular season in 1995. The Jaguars became the first NFL **expansion team** to play its first game in a brand-new stadium. A statue of a growling jaguar greets fans outside of the stadium's main entrance.

BY THE NUMBERS

- The Jaguars' stadium has 67,164 seats for football.
- It took just 20 months to build the stadium and cost $134 million.
- In 2005, the stadium hosted Super Bowl XXXIX between the New England Patriots and Philadelphia Eagles.

Fans pack into Jacksonville's stadium for a night game during the 2007 season.

Dressed for Success

The Jaguars' main uniform color is a shade of blue-green called teal. Other team colors include gold, black, and white. Jacksonville's first **logo** was a leaping jaguar. The big cat looked so much like the hood **ornament** for Jaguar automobiles that the team changed it. Jacksonville switched to a snarling jaguar head with a teal tongue. Before its first game with the new logo, the team handed out teal-colored candies so that all the fans would have the same color tongue as the jaguar.

The Jaguars wear black helmets and either white or teal jerseys. They added a black jersey in 2002. Because the weather in Florida can get very warm, Jacksonville usually wears its cooler white jerseys for home games early in the year. The Jaguars wear black pants or white pants. During the season, the team will use several combinations of jerseys and pants.

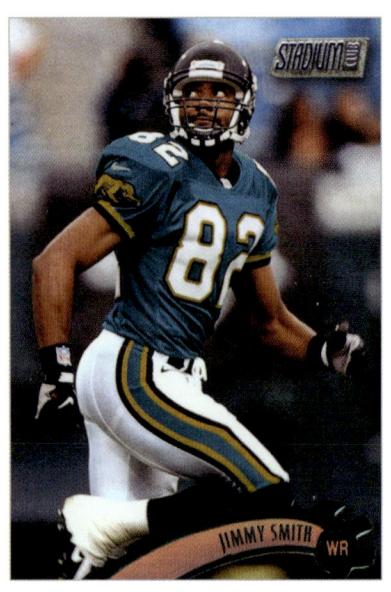

Jimmy Smith models the team's uniform from the 1990s.

UNIFORM BASICS

The football uniform has three important parts—
- Helmet
- Jersey
- Pants

Helmets used to be made out of leather, and they did not have facemasks—ouch! Today, helmets are made of super-strong plastic. The uniform top, or jersey, is made of thick fabric. It fits snugly around a player so that tacklers cannot grab it and pull him down. The pants come down just over the knees.

There is a lot more to a football uniform than what you see on the outside. Air can be pumped inside the helmet to give it a snug, padded fit. The jersey covers shoulder pads, and sometimes a rib protector called a flak jacket. The pants include pads that protect the hips, thighs, *tailbone*, and knees.

Football teams have two sets of uniforms—one dark and one light. This makes it easier to tell two teams apart on the field. Almost all teams wear their dark uniforms at home and their light ones on the road.

Maurice Jones-Drew wears the team's main home uniform for the 2007 season.

We Won!

Like all teams that join the NFL, the Jaguars started with many players who had been **overlooked** by other clubs. For example, Jimmy Smith was cut by the Dallas Cowboys and Philadelphia Eagles. Other players, such as Mark Brunell, had been

stuck behind good players on other teams. Brunell was the backup quarterback for the Green Bay Packers. Their starter, Brett Favre, never missed a game!

Unlike other new teams, the Jaguars became winners almost right away. Coach Tom Coughlin knew what it took to be successful in the NFL, and he knew how to get the most out of his players. In their second season, the Jaguars started believing in themselves and made the playoffs on the last day of the season. In their final game, they led the Atlanta Falcons 19–17 with time running out. The Falcons had a chance to kick the winning field goal. Jaguars fans held their breath as the ball headed for the goal posts—and then drifted wide.

Jacksonville's first playoff game came a week later in Buffalo against the Bills. The Jaguars faced a tough battle. The Bills were 9–0 in playoff games in their stadium. Early in the game, Buffalo quarterback Jim Kelly tried a short pass. Defensive end Clyde Simmons snatched it out of the air and ran for a touchdown. Suddenly, the Jaguars realized they could beat this team. They played hard and won on a field goal by Mike Hollis. The kick banged off one of the goal posts before bouncing through.

LEFT: Mark Brunell drops back to pass against the Atlanta Falcons.
ABOVE: Clyde Simmons rumbles for his touchdown against the Buffalo Bills.

The following weekend, the Jaguars traveled to Denver to play the Broncos. Denver had the best record and the best defense in the AFC. It made no difference to the Jaguars. After falling behind 12–0, they scored on six possessions in a row on their way to a 30–27 victory.

Unfortunately, Jacksonville's amazing run ended in the AFC Championship game. The Jaguars lost 20–6 to the New England Patriots. Jacksonville fans were still proud of their team.

The Jaguars reached the conference championship game again in 1999. This time, it was Jacksonville that had the AFC's best record and toughest defense. The Jaguars proved it in their opening playoff games against the Miami Dolphins. They rolled to a 62–7 victory. The Jaguars looked like they were headed to the Super Bowl, until they ran into the Tennessee Titans. Jacksonville lost 33–14. The team was disappointed, but it knew the Super Bowl was within reach.

LEFT: Jimmy Smith is congratulated by Pete Mitchell after a touchdown against the Denver Broncos.   **ABOVE**: The scoreboard tells the story in Jacksonville's win over the Miami Dolphins.

Go-To Guys

To be a true star in the NFL, you need more than fast feet and a big body. You have to be a "go-to guy"—someone the coach wants on the field at the end of a big game. Jaguars fans have had a lot to cheer about over the years, including these great stars …

THE PIONEERS

TONY BOSELLI — Offensive Lineman

- BORN: 4/17/1972   • PLAYED FOR TEAM: 1995 TO 2001

Tony Boselli was the first draft pick of the Jaguars. He was an excellent athlete who stood 6′ 7″ and weighed 325 pounds. Boselli was the top-rated left tackle in the NFL for many years. The Jaguars had a lot of success running behind him during the 1990s.

MARK BRUNELL — Quarterback

- BORN: 9/17/1970   • PLAYED FOR TEAM: 1995 TO 2003

Mark Brunell spent one year as a backup before the Green Bay Packers traded him to Jacksonville. Brunell was a great leader who never *panicked*. He was especially good when the defense forced him to scramble. Brunell played in the **Pro Bowl** three times for the Jaguars.

JIMMY SMITH — Receiver

- BORN: 2/9/1969   • PLAYED FOR TEAM: 1995 TO 2005

Jimmy Smith had great speed, soft hands, and a quick mind—the perfect combination for a receiver. He was a big reason the Jaguars made it to the AFC Championship game in 1999. That season, Smith led the NFL with 116 catches. He retired with 862 receptions and 68 touchdowns.

JAMES STEWART — Running Back

- BORN: 12/27/1971   • PLAYED FOR TEAM: 1995 TO 1999

James Stewart teamed with Natrone Means—and later Fred Taylor—to give the Jaguars a very good running attack. Stewart was also good at catching passes. He tied for the lead in the AFC with 13 rushing touchdowns in 1999.

MIKE HOLLIS — Kicker

- BORN: 5/22/1972   • PLAYED FOR TEAM: 1995 TO 2001

In seven seasons with the Jaguars, Mike Hollis scored nearly 800 points. He was a very accurate kicker who made 80 percent of his field goal attempts. In 1997, Hollis led the NFL with 134 points.

TONY BRACKENS — Defensive Lineman

- BORN: 12/26/1974   • PLAYED FOR TEAM: 1996 TO 2003

Tony Brackens was a quick and *agile* defender who made lots of big plays for the Jaguars. His best season came in 1999 when he had 12 **sacks**, returned an **interception** for a touchdown, and was named **All-Pro**.

LEFT: Tony Boselli
RIGHT: Tony Brackens

MODERN STARS

KEVIN HARDY — Linebacker

• Born: 7/24/1973   • Played for Team: 1996 to 2001

Kevin Hardy was Jacksonville's first pick in the 1996 draft. He was very good at rushing the quarterback and could also chase down running backs as they sprinted toward the sidelines. Hardy led the Jaguars in tackles in 1998 and 1999.

KEENAN McCARDELL — Receiver

• Born: 1/6/1970   • Played for Team: 1996 to 2001

The Jaguars signed Keenan McCardell to a contract even though he had started only 11 games in four years with the Cleveland Browns. McCardell was a big, fearless receiver who could take a hard tackle without losing the football. McCardell caught nearly 500 passes during his six seasons in Jacksonville.

FRED TAYLOR — Running Back

• Born: 1/27/1976   • First Season with Team: 1998

Fred Taylor had the power to break through tackles and the speed to outrun other defenders once he was in the open. Taylor passed the 10,000-yard mark for his career in 2007. After the season, he was selected to play in the Pro Bowl for the first time in his long career.

LEFT: Kevin Hardy
TOP RIGHT: Byron Leftwich
BOTTOM RIGHT: Maurice Jones-Drew

DAVID GARRARD   Quarterback

- **BORN**: 2/14/1978   • **FIRST SEASON WITH TEAM**: 2002

David Garrard hoped to follow Mark Brunell as Jacksonville's starting quarterback, but he ended up sitting on the bench behind Byron Leftwich. Garrard got his chance in 2007. He threw only three interceptions and led Jacksonville to the playoffs.

BYRON LEFTWICH   Quarterback

- **BORN**: 1/14/1980   • **PLAYED FOR TEAM**: 2003 TO 2006

Byron Leftwich became Jacksonville's starting quarterback during his **rookie** season. Though inexperienced, he won games with his creativity and toughness. Leftwich became one of the team's best leaders.

MAURICE JONES-DREW   Running Back

- **BORN**: 3/23/1985   • **FIRST SEASON WITH TEAM**: 2006

Maurice Jones-Drew was supposed to sit and learn from Fred Taylor when he joined the Jaguars. Instead, he scored touchdowns in eight games in a row as a rookie and finished with 16 for the season. Jones-Drew continued his excellent play in 2007.

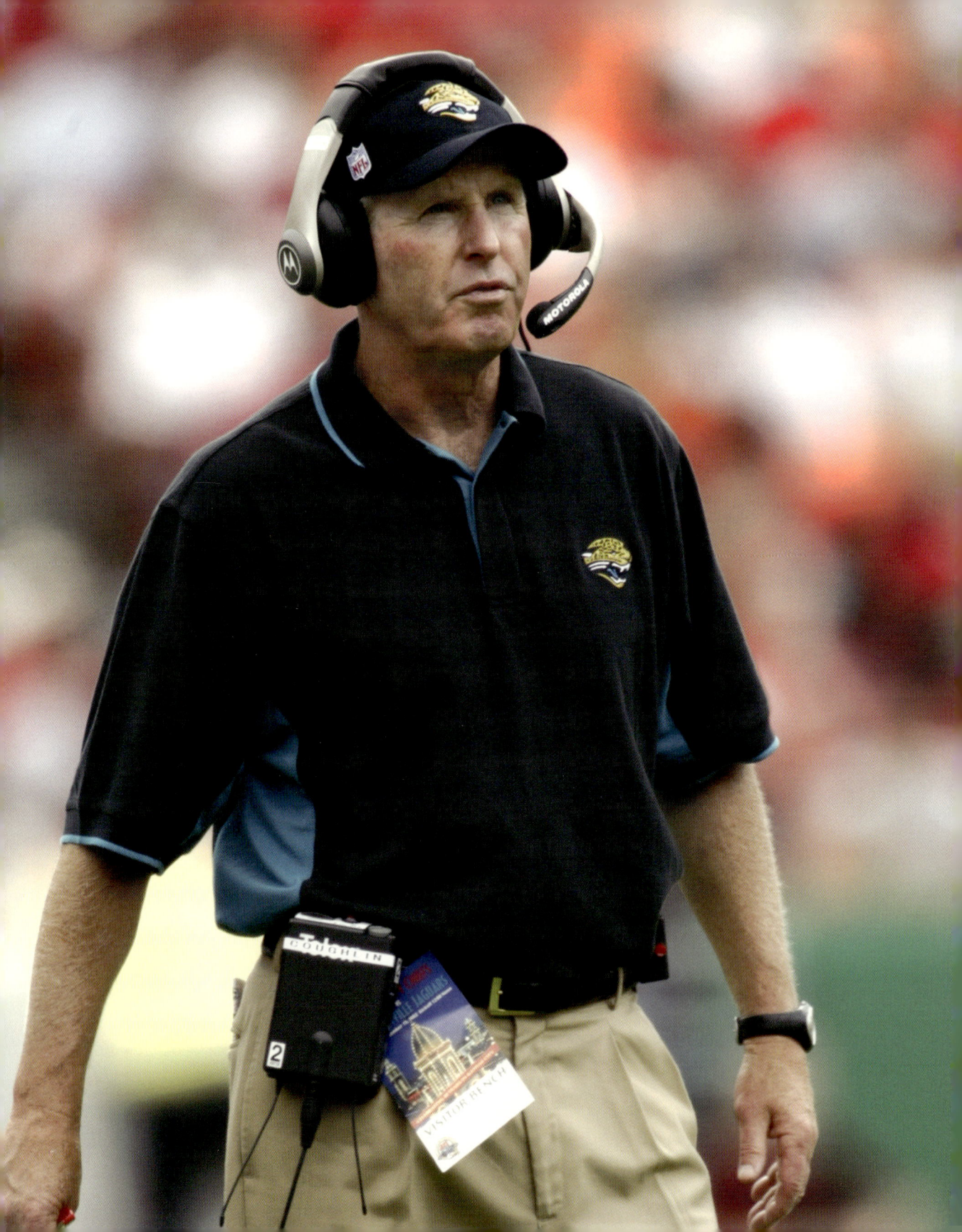

On the Sidelines

Jacksonville's first coach was Tom Coughlin. He had worked with receivers for many years in the NFL before becoming the head coach at Boston College. Coughlin turned the Jaguars into a great passing team. In Coughlin's second year with Jacksonville, Mark Brunell threw for more than 4,000 yards, and Jimmy Smith and Keenan McCardell each had more than 1,000 receiving yards. Under Coughlin, the Jaguars were the first expansion team to make the playoffs in four of their first five seasons.

In 2003, Jack Del Rio became the Jaguars' second head coach. Del Rio was a star linebacker in college and the NFL. After retiring, he coached the linebackers for the Baltimore Ravens. Soon after, Baltimore won the Super Bowl.

After Del Rio joined the Jaguars, he put a huge tree stump and an ax in the locker room—along with a sign that read, "Keep Chopping Wood." Del Rio believed team spirit was very important. This was his way of telling the players to work hard.

Tom Coughlin, the first coach in Jacksonville history.

One Great Day

JANUARY 4, 1997

When the 1996 regular season ended, the Jaguars were one of the hottest teams in football. In just their second year, they had made the playoffs by winning their last five games in a row. No one was sure how Jacksonville would do in the **postseason**. The team survived its first playoff game, against the Buffalo Bills. Would their luck hold out against John Elway and the mighty Denver Broncos?

It looked bad for the Jaguars in the first quarter. They did not make a single first down. The Broncos, meanwhile, scored 12 points on two touchdowns. The Jaguars blocked the extra point after the first, and then stopped a **two-point conversion** on the next. No one knew it then, but the Broncos would end up needing those points.

Starting in the second quarter, the Jaguars scored the next six times they had the ball. Natrone Means, Keenan McCardell, and Jimmy

Smith crossed the goal line for touchdowns, and Mike Hollis kicked three field goals to give Jacksonville a 30–20 lead in the fourth quarter. On the team's final touchdown drive, Mark Brunell made a great play. With the Jaguars facing an important fourth down, he scrambled for 29 yards.

The Broncos came roaring back to make the score 30–27, but the Jacksonville defense forced them to waste too much time on the clock. The Jaguars—a **Wild Card** team in its first postseason—had beaten the team with the AFC's best record and most talented quarterback.

LEFT: Natrone Means looks for an opening against the Denver Broncos.
ABOVE: Mark Brunell, whose great scrambling helped the Jaguars seal their victory.

Legend Has It

Which Jaguars runner had Hall of Fame statistics?

LEGEND HAS IT that Fred Taylor did. From 1998 to 2007, Taylor gained 1,000 yards or more seven times. Heading into 2008, he had a career average of 4.7 yards per carry. Joe Perry, Jim Brown, and Barry Sanders were the only players with a better average. All three are in the **Hall of Fame**. Will Taylor make it there, too? Only time will tell. He finally made it to his first Pro Bowl after 10 seasons in the NFL, when he was asked to replace an injured player.

ABOVE: Fred Taylor jogs onto the field before a game.
RIGHT: Jack Del Rio wears his famous suit.

Who owns the most famous suit in Florida?

LEGEND HAS IT that Jack Del Rio does. Since the early 1990s, the NFL has asked its coaches to wear sideline gear in official team colors. In November 2006, Del Rio decided to wear a suit and tie for a game against the New York Giants. The Jaguars won 26–10. He wore a suit again in December for a game against the Indianapolis Colts. The Jaguars did even better—they beat Indianapolis 44–17. The fans wanted Del Rio to wear a suit and tie at every home game in 2007, and the NFL said OK!

Which two Jaguars took the NFL by "storm" in 1996?

LEGEND HAS IT that Keenan McCardell and Jimmy Smith did. They were nicknamed "Thunder & Lightning." McCardell was a big receiver who *thundered* across the field after catching passes. Smith was as fast as lightning—once he got past a defender, there was no way to catch him. In 1996, McCardell caught 85 passes for 1,129 yards, and Smith caught 83 passes for 1,244 yards.

It Really Happened

The 1999 AFC playoffs were supposed to be the final farewell for Dan Marino of the Miami Dolphins. The record-smashing quarterback planned to retire after the season. Some of his fans thought he might lead his team to the Super Bowl. The Jaguars had other plans for the Dolphins.

Coach Tom Coughlin told the Jacksonville players that they had to **seize** control of the game in the first quarter. They could not afford to let Marino get into a groove. The Jaguars did exactly as they were instructed. Before the Dolphins scored a single point, Mark Brunell had thrown a touchdown pass to Jimmy Smith, Mike Hollis had kicked a field goal, Fred Taylor scored on a long run, and Tony Brackens picked up a **fumble** and ran it into the end zone. After 15 minutes, the Jaguars were ahead 24–0!

Taylor's run hurt the Dolphins the most. It seemed to take the fight out of them. Taylor

broke through the line deep in Jacksonville territory, and then sprinted 90 yards for a touchdown. It was the longest running play in the history of the playoffs.

Later in the game, Taylor scored another touchdown, this time on a pass from Brunell. In the fourth quarter, Jay Fiedler replaced Brunell and passed for a touchdown. The final score was 62–7.

Jacksonville had put up the most points ever by an AFC team in the playoffs. The Jaguars had also set a team record for scoring, and the Dolphins had never been beaten so badly.

LEFT: The Jaguars pounded Dan Marino early and often in their 1999 playoff matchup.   **ABOVE**: Fred Taylor runs by a defender for the Miami Dolphins.

Team Spirit

The Jaguars may be one of the newer teams in sports, but their fans are old pros when it comes to football. They know the game inside-out, and win or lose, they show the Jaguars a lot of love for their effort. That is a big reason why the players enjoy living and playing in the Jacksonville area.

The team also goes all-out when it comes to entertaining the fans. The Jacksonville D-Line is the official drumline of the Jaguars. Drumlines have a great history in football, especially in the South. Fans who attend college football games like that they can find this same tradition in an NFL stadium.

The coolest cat in Jacksonville is Jaxson de Ville, the team's **mascot**. The fans love it when he dances to the song "Stray Cat Strut." Both Jaxson and the D-Line perform all over northern Florida between games and after each season.

Reggie Williams jumps into the stands to celebrate a touchdown with Jacksonville fans during a 2007 game.

Timeline

In this timeline, the Pro Bowl is listed under the year it was played. Remember that the Pro Bowl is held early in the year and is actually part of the previous season. For example, the 2008 Pro Bowl was played in February, but it recognized the top players from the 2007 NFL season.

1995
The Jaguars go 4–12 in their first season.

1999
Jimmy Smith leads the NFL with 116 catches.

1993
The NFL announces Jacksonville as its 30th team.

1996
The Jaguars win their last five games to make the playoffs.

1998
The Jaguars are **AFC Central** champions for the first time.

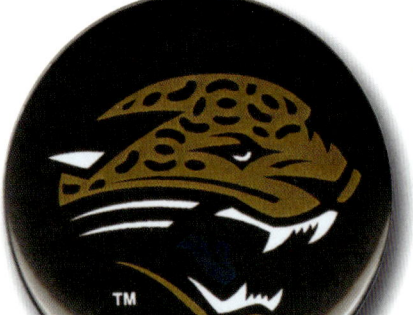

A souvenir pin from the team's first season.

Tony Boselli, a leader on the 1998 champs.

Maurice Jones-Drew runs for a touchdown in 2006.

2003
Jack Del Rio becomes Jacksonville's head coach.

2006
Maurice Jones-Drew tops all rookies with 16 touchdowns.

2002
The Jaguars move to the new **AFC South** Division.

2007
Reggie Nelson ties for the most interceptions among NFL rookies.

2008
Fred Taylor plays in his first Pro Bowl.

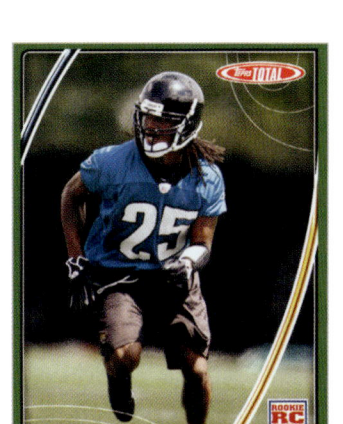

Reggie Nelson

Fred Taylor

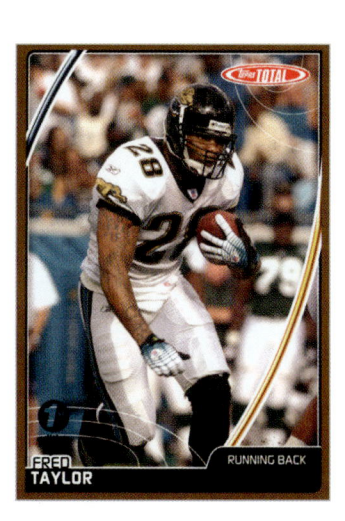

Fun Facts

GUTTING IT OUT

When David Garrard became the starting quarterback in 2007, he was grateful for the opportunity—and happy to be alive. Three years earlier, doctors told him he had **Crohn's disease**. Garrard had major **intestinal** surgery but still played in four games during the 2004 season.

PURR-FECT

When the Jaguars wanted an official team car, they called—who else?—Jaguar Motors. The company was happy to supply them with automobiles in exchange for free advertising!

MAMA'S BOY

One of the first players Tom Coughlin signed in 1995 was Jimmy Smith. How did Coughlin know about the speedy receiver? Smith's mother had sent him a scrapbook full of her son's press clippings.

FAST COMPANY

In 2000, Fred Taylor recovered from an early-season injury to gain more than 100 yards nine games in a row. Barry Sanders (14) and Marcus Allen (11) were the only players in history with longer streaks.

BLOCK PARTY

In 2006, Jacksonville's offensive linemen enjoyed an amazing year. The Jaguars set team rushing records with 2,541 yards in a season and 375 yards in a game. A year later, the offensive line did its job again when quarterback David Garrard was pressured into just three interceptions.

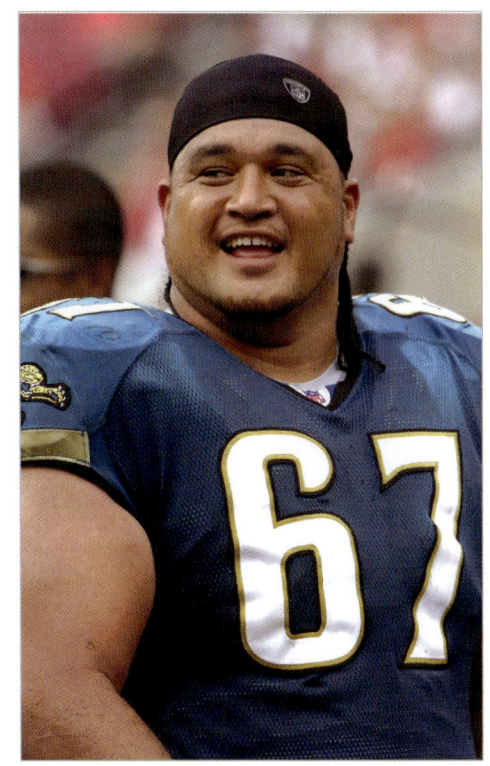

WHO WANTS TO PLAY?

Before the Jaguars came to town, Jacksonville tried to talk the Baltimore Colts and Houston Oilers into moving to Florida. The city had pro teams in the **World Football League (WFL)** and **United States Football League (USFL)**, but both leagues went out of business.

LEFT: David Garrard   **ABOVE**: Vince Manuwai, a star on Jacksonville's great offensive line in 2006 and 2007.

Talking Football

"I always come into the game wanting the ball."
—Fred Taylor, on how he gets ready to play

"He's a real physical football player. He's a good **blocker**. He plays the whole game."
—Jack Del Rio, on Maurice Jones-Drew

"We've got a saying around here: 'Don't blink because you never know what's going to happen.'"
—Rashean Mathis, on always being alert on the field

"When I watch film of myself, I look to see if I do what I'm supposed to do consistently."
—Tony Boselli, on preparing for games away from the field

ABOVE: Rashean Mathis
RIGHT: Keenan McCardell

"When we get into a rhythm, we're hard to stop."
— *Keenan McCardell, on the Jaguars from 1996 to 2001*

"There's definitely added pressure. But it's how you manage and how you deal with that pressure."
— *David Garrard, on becoming a starting quarterback*

"If I'm going to play, it's got to be 100 percent. I won't get out there and not give it my all."
— *Jimmy Smith, on giving his best on every play*

"Without question, of the players available, he was the guy I wanted to be the quarterback of the future."
— *Tom Coughlin, on Mark Brunell*

For the Record

The great Jaguars teams and players have left their marks on the record books. These are the "best of the best" ...

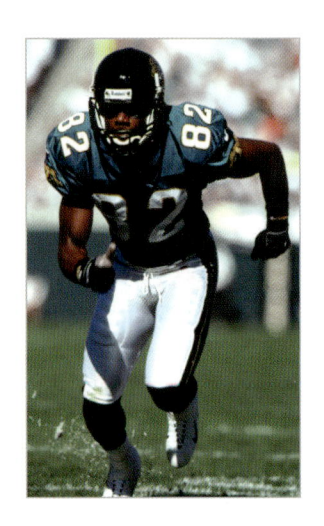

JAGUARS AWARD WINNERS

WINNER	AWARD	YEAR
Mark Brunell	Pro Bowl Most Valuable Player*	1997

An award given to the best player in the NFL's annual all-star game.

JAGUARS ACHIEVEMENTS

AFC Central Champions	1998
AFC Central Champions	1999

TOP LEFT: Jimmy Smith, the team's top receiver in 1998.
BOTTOM LEFT: James Stewart, the team's top rusher in 1999.
RIGHT: Mark Brunell looks for a receiver during the 1997 Pro Bowl.

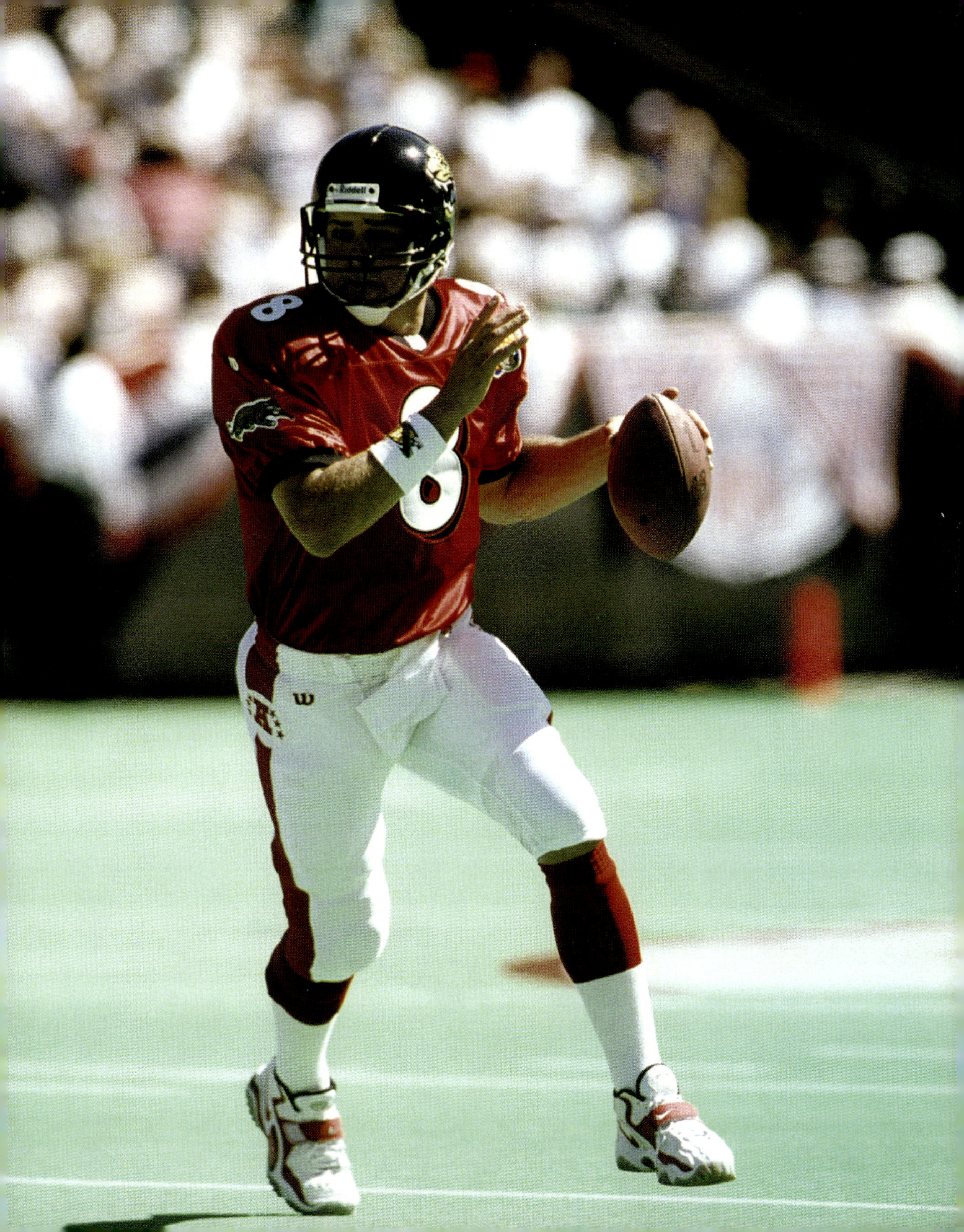
Riddell

Pinpoints

The history of a football team is made up of many smaller stories. These stories take place all over the map—not just in the city a team calls "home." Match the pushpins on these maps to the Team Facts and you will begin to see the story of the Jaguars unfold!

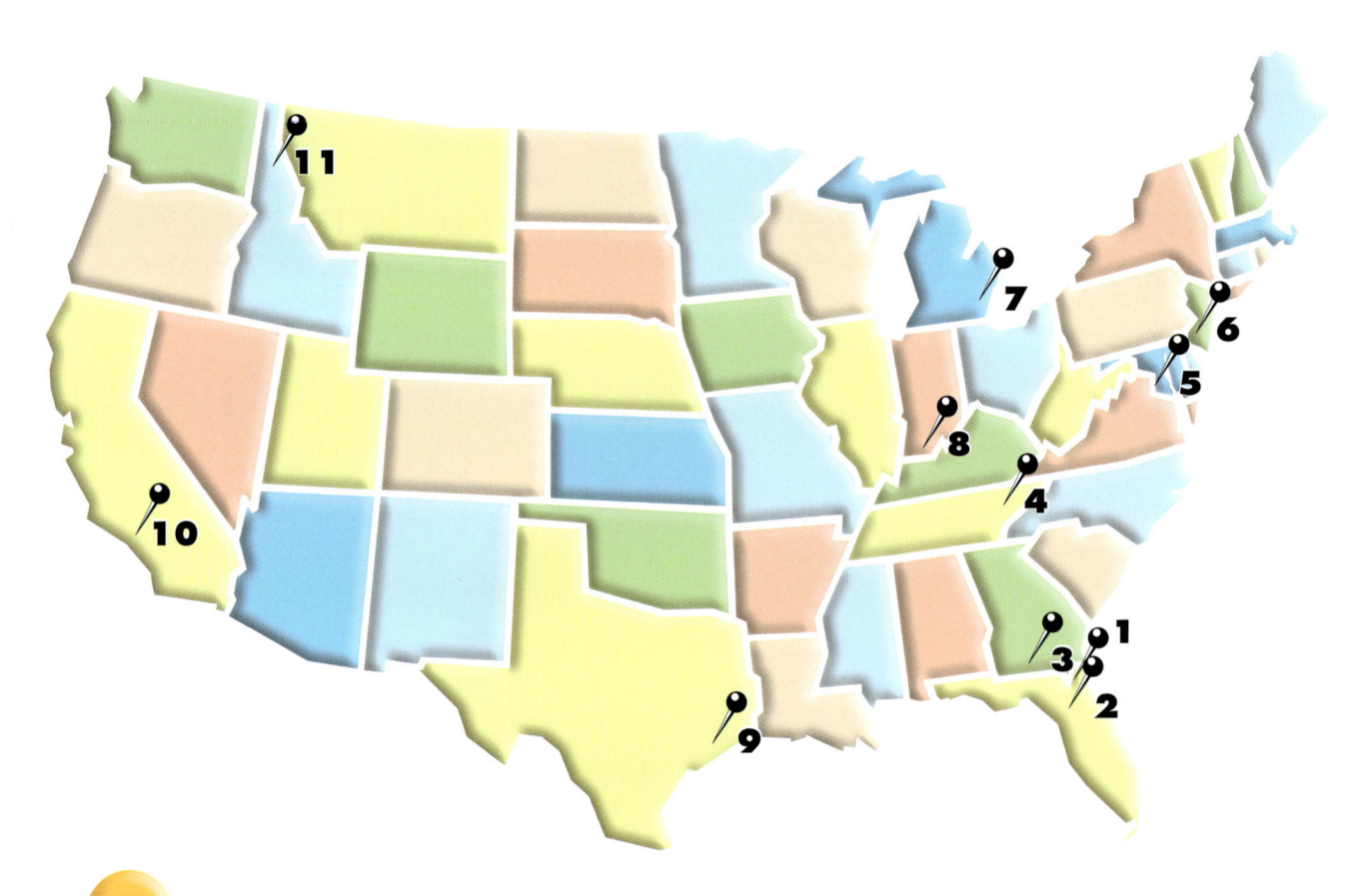

TEAM FACTS

1 Jacksonville, Florida—*The team has played here since 1995.*
2 Gainesville, Florida—*Mike Peterson was born here.*
3 Thomasville, Georgia—*Marcus Stroud was born here.*
4 Morristown, Tennessee—*James Stewart was born here.*
5 Washington, D.C.—*Byron Leftwich was born here.*
6 Camden, New Jersey—*Donovin Darius was born here.*
7 Detroit, Michigan—*Jimmy Smith was born here.*
8 Evansville, Indiana—*Kevin Hardy was born here.*
9 Houston, Texas—*Keenan McCardell was born here.*
10 Los Angeles, California—*Mark Brunell was born here.*
11 Kellogg, Idaho—*Mike Hollis was born here.*
12 Honolulu, Hawaii—*Vince Manuwai was born here.*

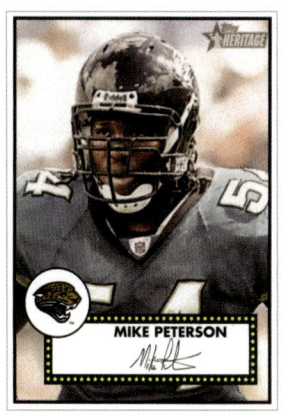

Mike Peterson

43

Play Ball

Football is a sport played by two teams on a field that is 100 yards long. The game is divided into four 15-minute quarters. Each team must have 11 players on the field at all times. The group that has the ball is called the offense. The group trying to keep the offense from moving the ball forward is called the defense.

A football game is made up of a series of "plays." Each play starts and ends with a referee's signal. A play begins when the center snaps the ball between his legs to the quarterback. The quarterback then gives the ball to a teammate, throws (or "passes") the ball to a teammate, or runs with the ball himself. The job of the defense is to tackle the player with the ball or stop the quarterback's pass. A play ends when the ball (or player holding the ball) is "down." The offense must move the ball forward at least 10 yards every four downs. If it fails to do so, the other team is given the ball. If the offense has not made 10 yards after three downs—and does not want to risk losing the ball—it can kick (or "punt") the ball to make the other team start from its own end of the field.

At each end of a football field is a goal line, which divides the field from the end zone. A team must run or pass the ball over the goal line to score a touchdown, which counts for six points. After scoring a touchdown, a team can try a short kick for one "extra point," or try again to run or pass across the goal line for two points. Teams can score three points from anywhere on the field by kicking the ball between the goal posts. This is called a field goal.

The defense can score two points if it tackles a player while he is in his own end zone. This is called a safety. The defense can also score points by taking the ball away from the offense and crossing the opposite goal line for a touchdown. The team with the most points after 60 minutes is the winner.

Football may seem like a very hard game to understand, but the more you play and watch football, the more "little things" you are likely to notice. The next time you are at a game, look for these plays:

PLAY LIST

BLITZ—A play where the defense sends extra tacklers after the quarterback. If the quarterback sees a blitz coming, he passes the ball quickly. If he does not, he can end up at the bottom of a very big pile!

DRAW—A play where the offense pretends it will pass the ball, and then gives it to a running back. If the offense can "draw" the defense to the quarterback and his receivers, the running back should have lots of room to run.

FLY PATTERN—A play where a team's fastest receiver is told to "fly" past the defensive backs for a long pass. Many long touchdowns are scored on this play.

SQUIB KICK—A play where the ball is kicked a short distance on purpose. A squib kick is used when the team kicking off does not want the other team's fastest player to catch the ball and run with it.

SWEEP—A play where the ball carrier follows a group of teammates moving sideways to "sweep" the defense out of the way. A good sweep gives the runner a chance to gain a lot of yards before he is tackled or forced out of bounds.

Glossary

FOOTBALL WORDS TO KNOW

AFC CENTRAL—A division for teams that play in the central part of the country.

AFC CHAMPIONSHIP—The game played to determine which AFC team will go to the Super Bowl.

AFC SOUTH—A division for teams that play in the southern part of the country.

ALL-PRO—An honor given to the best players at their position at the end of each season.

AMERICAN FOOTBALL CONFERENCE (AFC)—One of two groups of teams that make up the NFL. The winner of the AFC plays the winner of the National Football Conference (NFC) in the Super Bowl.

BLOCKER—A player who protects the ball carrier with his body.

DRAFT PICK—A college player selected or "drafted" by an NFL team each spring.

EXPANSION TEAM—A team added to a league when it expands.

FREE AGENT—A player who is allowed to sign with any team that wants him.

FUMBLE—A ball that is dropped by the player carrying it.

HALL OF FAME—The museum in Canton, Ohio, where football's greatest players are honored. A player voted into the Hall of Fame is sometimes called a "Hall of Famer."

INTERCEPTION—A pass that is caught by the defensive team.

NATIONAL FOOTBALL LEAGUE (NFL)—The league that started in 1920 and is still operating today.

PLAYOFFS—The games played after the season to determine which teams play in the Super Bowl.

POSTSEASON—Another term for playoffs.

PRO BOWL—The NFL's all-star game, played after the Super Bowl.

PROFESSIONAL—A player or team that plays a sport for money.

ROOKIE—A player in his first season.

SACKS—Tackles of the quarterback behind the line of scrimmage.

SEASON TICKETS—Packages of tickets for each home game.

SUPER BOWL—The championship of football, played between the winners of the NFC and AFC.

TWO-POINT CONVERSION—A play following a touchdown where the offense tries to cross the goal line with the ball from the 2 yard line, instead of kicking an extra point.

UNITED STATES FOOTBALL LEAGUE (USFL)—The league that tried to challenge the NFL in the 1980s. The USFL started in 1983 and ended in 1985.

WILD CARD—A team that makes the playoffs without winning its division.

WORLD FOOTBALL LEAGUE (WFL)—The league that tried to challenge the NFL in the 1970s. The WFL started in 1974 and ended in 1975.

OTHER WORDS TO KNOW

AGILE—Quick and graceful.

CENTURY—A period of 100 years.

CONTAGIOUS—Spread easily from one person to another.

CONTENDER—A team that competes for a championship.

CROHN'S DISEASE—An illness that affects the intestines.

FORMULA—A set way of doing something.

INTESTINAL—Having to do with the digestive system.

LOGO—A symbol or design that represents a company or team.

MASCOT—An animal or person believed to bring a group good luck.

ORNAMENT—Something used as a decoration.

OVERLOOKED—Failed to see or notice.

PANICKED—Got nervous.

SEIZE—Capture or gain.

SENSATIONAL—Amazing.

TAILBONE—The bone that protects the base of the spine.

THUNDERED—Moved with great force.

TRADITION—A belief or custom that is handed down from generation to generation.

Places to Go

ON THE ROAD

JACKSONVILLE JAGUARS
One ALLTEL Stadium Place
Jacksonville, Florida 32202
(904) 633-6000

THE PRO FOOTBALL HALL OF FAME
2121 George Halas Drive NW
Canton, Ohio 44708
(330) 456-8207

ON THE WEB

THE NATIONAL FOOTBALL LEAGUE   www.nfl.com
• *Learn more about the National Football League*

THE JACKSONVILLE JAGUARS   www.jaguars.com
• *Learn more about the Jaguars*

THE PRO FOOTBALL HALL OF FAME   www.profootballhof.com
• *Learn more about football's greatest players*

ON THE BOOKSHELF

To learn more about the sport of football, look for these books at your library or bookstore:

- Fleder, Rob–Editor. *The Football Book*. New York, New York: Sports Illustrated Books, 2005.
- Kennedy, Mike. *Football*. Danbury, Connecticut: Franklin Watts, 2003.
- Savage, Jeff. *Play by Play Football*. Minneapolis, Minnesota: Lerner Sports, 2004.

Index

PAGE NUMBERS IN **BOLD** REFER TO ILLUSTRATIONS.

Allen, Marcus	37	Manuwai, Vince	**37**, 43
Boselli, Tony	6, 20, **20**, **34**, 38	Marino, Dan	30, **30**
Brackens, Tony	9, 21, **21**, 30	Mathis, Rashean	11, 38, **38**
Brown, Jim	28	McCardell, Keenan	7, **7**, 22, 25, 26, 29, 39, **39**, 43
Brunell, Mark	6, **6**, 7, 16, **16**, 20, 23, 25, 27, **27**, 30, 31, 39, 40, **41**, 43	Means, Natrone	7, 21, 26, **26**
Coughlin, Tom	6, **6**, 16, **24**, 25, 30, 36, 39	Mitchell, Pete	**18**
		Nelson, Reggie	11, 35, **35**
		Paup, Bryce	9
Darius, Donovin	9, 43	Perry, Joe	28
Del Rio, Jack	9, 25, 29, **29**, 35, 38	Peterson, Mike	11, 43, **43**
Elway, John	26	Porter, Jerry	11
Favre, Brett	16	Sanders, Barry	28, 37
Fiedler, Jay	31	Simmons, Clyde	17, **17**
Garrard, David	**10**, 11, 23, 36, **36**, 37, 39	Smith, Jimmy	7, **7**, 11, **14**, 16, **18**, 21, 25, 27, 29, 30, 34, 36, 39, **40**, 43
Gator Bowl	13		
Hardy, Kevin	9, 22, **22**, 43		
Hollis, Mike	17, 21, 27, 30, 43	Stewart, James	6, 21, **40**, 43
Jacksonville Municipal Stadium	**12**, 13	Stroud, Marcus	9, 43
		Taylor, Fred	**4**, **8**, 9, **10**, 11, 21, 22, 23, 28, **28**, 30, 31, **31**, 35, **35**, 37, 38
Jones-Drew, Maurice	11, **15**, 23, **23**, 35, **35**, 38		
Kelly, Jim	17		
Lake, Carnell	9	Weaver, J. Wayne	6
Leftwich, Byron	23, **23**, 43	Williams, Reggie	11, **32**

The Team

MARK STEWART has written more than 20 books on football, and over 100 sports books for kids. He grew up in New York City during the 1960s rooting for the Giants and Jets, and now takes his two daughters, Mariah and Rachel, to watch them play in their home state of New Jersey. Mark comes from a family of writers. His grandfather was Sunday Editor of *The New York Times* and his mother was Articles Editor of *The Ladies' Home Journal* and *McCall's*. Mark has profiled hundreds of athletes over the last 20 years. He has also written several books about New York and New Jersey. Mark is a graduate of Duke University, with a degree in History. He lives with his daughters and wife Sarah overlooking Sandy Hook, New Jersey.

JASON AIKENS is the Collections Curator at the Pro Football Hall of Fame. He is responsible for the preservation of the Pro Football Hall of Fame's collection of artifacts and memorabilia and obtaining new donations of memorabilia from current players and NFL teams. Jason has a Bachelor of Arts in History from Michigan State University and a Master's in History from Western Michigan University where he concentrated on sports history. Jason has been working for the Pro Football Hall of Fame since 1997; before that he was an intern at the College Football Hall of Fame. Jason's family has roots in California and has been following the St. Louis Rams since their days in Los Angeles, California. He lives with his wife Cynthia and their daughter Angelina in Canton, Ohio.